I0772394

scavengers

"I am listening in the dark
to hear what comes after

grief collapses time
between us: a body pulled

from its ache into daylight.
It's nothing if not grotesque.

And some of us look away
and some of us want to watch."

—Allison Titus, High Lonesome

CONTENTS

neither bear, nor man

    —Alexandria Piette

women must choose between bear and man, and i wonder why they must succumb to threat in every story. *let them choose the earth.* let them not be the horror-stricken meat whose inner depths are eaten first, arteries slick with the violence of ancestry where all the waning heartbeat knows is burn, stone, plead. let them choose the bluegrass, the butterfly weeds, the blanketflowers to warm the biting forest gloaming. let them peer up into the branches of the sycamore trees, drowning in sunlight through the turn of cadmium green smothering the last of the cheerless blues of february. let their flesh be held adoringly by the tide of the lake, the insatiable yearning to explore beyond the buoys. in the ending to this, let them be reminded there is no taking. give as they might, no creature can come between the vicious resistance of a mother and her nature. birthstone, star sign, birth flower, moon phase, planets aligning like a cosmic consecration—a woman is born and bred within it all.

—Alexandria Piette—

this will destroy you
—Alexandra Piette

my freshly updated medical history reads, "mixed obsessional thoughts and acts." i picture my psychiatrist typing thoughtfully, taking care with each letter forming a sentence, a penalty. my mother shares a grainy photograph from a late 2000's digital camera of my childhood; see the bathroom sink, see toothpaste, floss, deodorant, hand soap, hand sanitizer—all lined atop the laminate counter next to a stereo that croons with cd mixes. see hairbrush, hairspray just behind it, brunette ponytail pulled taut like muscles, knots along my back, twisted into a chignon and coated in product. my friends gift me tin bottles of hairspray for christmas and we laugh through bumbling braces, rib-tickling girlhood. a hairstylist trims my tresses, noticing the breakage like i took shears to the underside of my skull. *what happened?* i don't tell her my father recently married a woman who pours boxed wine with every meal, that i don't sleep until the sun dawns every other weekend. *i wear my hair up a lot.* see mouthwash, passionfruit perfume, strawberry lipgloss, glitter on my cheekbones. i wear the same navy-blue cardigan to school most mornings, in one-hundred-degree florida heat. he makes me turkey and cheese sandwiches on saturdays at noon, sets ceramic on the glass of the coffee table, me on the verdant carpet like a forest i would go missing in. *ceiling, plate, up, down.* only then can i bite into it, let it somersault across my tongue. *what about now?* let me tell you. i read the title of the book, author, spine, title, author. the thoughts whir inside me like a suburban lawn mower slicing through wheatgrass. *what if you—? what if i—?* a doctor at the hospital says, *tell me about these intrusions.* my face feels like a desert sun, oasis miles past saving. i want to catapult his keyboard into the hardwood, clutch his shoulders, shake him when i declare, *they are things i would never do.* how to eradicate it like a virus, balance in the brain zombified, the end is near. *toothpaste, floss; ceiling, plate; title, author.* how to destroy the soundness.

Oriónidas
  —Duna Haller

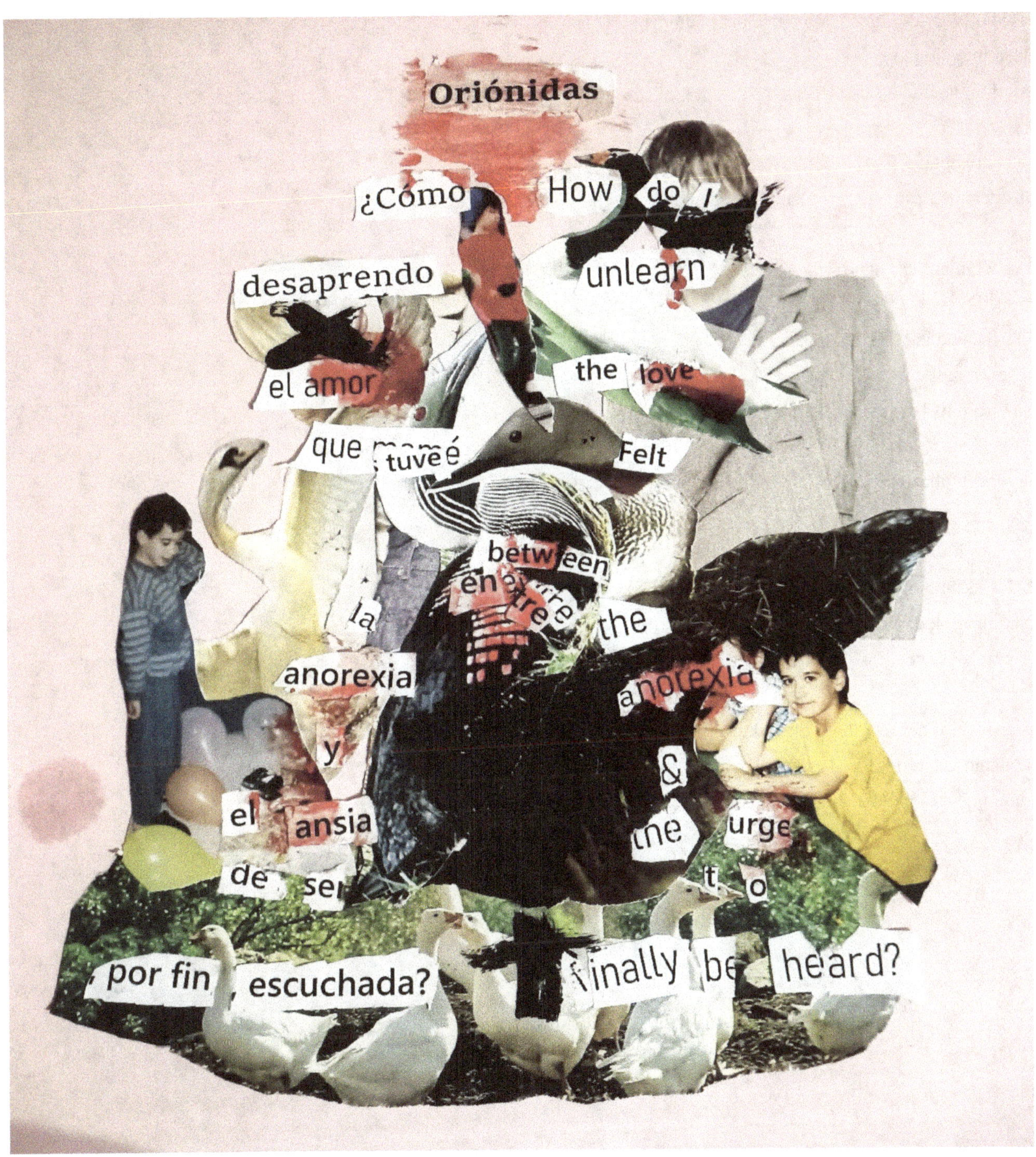

—Duna Haller—

When a poet dreams about Judy Chicago eating an apple
  —Sophia Murray

peeled   sliced   perfection
Raised on a gold gilded edge porcelain platter
placed intentionally
central to the mind's eye

She contemplates it
Considers its flesh   shape   context

The peel in her left hand
wrapped around her knuckles
flicks the end in time to a tick
The knife in her right
moist from its latest victim

She renders the apple edible   suitable
Pierced
she raises it to her lips
Inhales its sinning scent
in anticipation of a bite
Her purple stained lips part green on lilac

The garden of her mouth met with hunger waters
She abandons it to the gallery floor
A monument to the defiance of expectations

—Sophia Murray—

SELF-PORTRAIT WITH EYES
—Annaliese Jakimides

—Annaliese Jakimides—

The Intruder

—Jay Ponteri

My son wears headphones a lot of the time while we sit on the couch, him working on his laptop on schoolwork and me watching tennis and making my ongoing commentary about the players, the courts, the computer line-calling system, the commentators themselves and his not hearing a word I'm saying—I'm having a conversation with myself. I begin moving my mouth as if I were speaking, lip syncing words and gesticulating dramatically so that when he lifts his headphones off his head to hear what I'm saying, he encounters exactly what he encountered before taking off his headphones. I have been doing these little jocular performances since he was born and we do like to laugh a lot together. Later that night I'm in bed with MO the pug (for whom I'm also doing little performances) and I decide that I will give my son a little extra time in the morning to sleep by taking out MO for his walk and I call out to my son to let him know, I call his name three times and he doesn't respond and then I imagine me doing this in 18 months, calling out his name and hearing no response not because he's wearing his headphones and cannot hear me but because he's not here, he's moved out, and then I imagine my mom calling my name, calling my brother's names, each one after the next. And, of course, at this moment I'm not able to imagine the reality that after my son leaves for college, I'll awake from recurring nightmares in which someone has walked into my apartment in the middle of the night—an intruder? Him coming home from a night out with friends?—and in response I say his name again and again, eventually screaming myself awake.

Anxiety

—*Jay Ponteri*

I didn't locate the cotton swab at the end of my fingertips nor did I see it on the bathroom floor tiles because it was still falling through the air.

James and Ella

—Jay Ponteri

James and Ella move into the apartment next door. They are young, in their 20s. Ella is a nursing student at the University hospital on the hill while James works remotely for a marketing firm. Over the first couple days, we say hello to each other, we recall one another's names. James mentions he likes to play music that I might hear through our shared wall and if the music is too loud I can let him know and I tell him he will not hear much at all from my side other than my son infrequently yelling at the players of his beloved Phoenix Suns. James and Ella decorate our shared front porch with a variety of plants. We come and go from our apartments around the same time, mid-morning and late afternoon, and we make sure to close our front doors gently, quietly. They ask me what I do and express interest in my job; they mention they have taken note of my IBM Selectric, which you can see through the front window. In short, we become *good* neighbors, friendly, caring, curious. Eventually they invite people over for a party and I hear footsteps on the staircase up to our shared front porch, their door opening and closing, voices laughing and exclaiming and music pours through our shared wall. Another day I see them on the front porch with two suitcases—they're headed to the coast for the weekend. If there's a package outside their front door, I'll grab it and bring it over when they return. I think, *A puppy will be coming into this picture soon.* On weekends James returns with a six-pack of cider or a carton of eggs. On week nights, Ella returns wearing blue scrubs, looking exhausted, relieved to return to their new home. I can feel their love for each other, feel the ease with which they're settling into a shared life. It's hard not to imagine the rest—the puppy, family visiting them ("Let's go see the kids in Portland."), graduation for Ella, promotions and career development for both, eventually buying a house and getting married, traveling together when they can and when Ella's ready to go through pregnancy, one kid, eventually two, the quiet struggle with which they figure out how to split childcare duties, the holidays, the puppy so long from puppy hood, aches in its hips, the children performing with classmates in holiday plays crowded with teary-eyed, tired, parents… I realize I'm re-dreaming a happier version of my own difficult past, so I stop. Occasionally I do hear, coming through the wall we share, their music—and I wonder if they play it loudly during sex so they don't have to imagine me hearing the sounds their bodies make and, instead, can be focused on each other. As for me, I'm the perfect neighbor. James and Ella won't hear any sounds of fucking or loud music coming from my apartment. They might see me and my son heading out to grab a bite or one of us carrying my son's dog MO down the stairs so he doesn't reinjure his spine. Occasionally James puts on a record and plays it loudly—not a we-are-fucking record but just the two of them enjoying some music. Last night it was Tom Petty's *Wildflowers*, a divorce record if there ever were one, and I am imagining they're just tuning into the struggle—for all of our relationships are linked—the quiet melancholy that any marriage passes through, you are there, it's just the two of you and nobody else is coming over. It is not lost on me that I'm cheering for their relationship, for its meaning-making, its unfolding connectivity, and longevity, in ways I never cheered for, was unable to cheer for, mine. Also not lost on me is the mess of any loveship, how over the course of many years together any intimate relationship runs through many separations and reunions, how to share the struggles of their particular loops in ways that add depth to their connection, how to solve (or not) the puzzle of Jack Gilbert's line from his poem "The Great Fires"—*love lasts by not lasting.* Today as I walk up the porch stairs, I see a box of dog food outside their door and Ella, leaving for school, tells me the puppy arrives on Friday. I can't wait to meet it, I say.

333

—Jannat Alam

I once had a friend who drowned God under her tongue.

According to her, He tasted like 5-HTP and L-Theanine.

I get my horoscopes from license plates.

Joanne says I'm achieving my soul mission.

I wear pearls when I want to get something for nothing.

Did you know a cranial facial is just a lobotomy?

Here I am paying full price.

Apparently Sisyphus is going crazy on the rock now,

trying to crack it like a walnut. Good for him.

I'm still rolling fitfully in unlikely beds, painting

my nails just to chip them.

Possession can be soft.

The body is regrettably hard.

If only all break ups were like late night drives

to Pavement's "Newark Wilder."

Time can be spent like meaning can be approached:

outside a liquor store, emptying a blunt wrap,

mistaking rats for archangels,

track marks for constellations.

When a sparrow drops dead in front of you,

don't think of symbology.

Just bury it.

777

—Jannat Alam

You know they yoke beasts with men.
Give a code monkey a Substack, he'll
eventually get Heidegger's *Being and Time*.
Shoulder angels are just panoptics for kids; I
grew an eye in my brain in place of an amygdala.
Communication is based on exchange. For example,
trading a golden calf for a CA-compliant Ruger semi,
or a man that packs dip for the remaining detritus
of your twenties. Desire is carceral. A tiger falls
for a rat and the joke is that she wasn't short enough.
God gives his apes the burden of reflection all for a
little Saturday night entertainment--forgive me,
I was walking too noiselessly, what did you say?
That the onus of approximation is on the subject?
You really think so, buddy? At 3:27am BST, a monsoon
births an acid soluble only by blackgaze and cognitive
behavioral therapy: the line was already drawn, the snow
already white. You are your own stolen library copy.
It's all silly geese and stuck pigs until someone
tells you "No." Tell me, was there ever a way out
or were you just making that up?

Today Ghost
   —*Shaawan Francis Keahna*

—*Shaawan Francis Keahna*—

issues

      —finch greene

i.   there are always ghosts
      dancing in the corner of my eye.
      everything i'm afraid of
      is just close enough to reach,
      reminding me they can touch me
      whenever they want to.
      this empty is not romantic.
      this haunting is exhausting.

ii.   the man left me on read.
      i do love to have the last word,
      but there are so many things
      i wanted to say to him.
      no, him.
      no, him.
      no, to my dad. of course
      every man who has ever hurt me
      becomes my dad. i'm left
      carrying my own heavy mouth.

iii.   good things take time.
      or, the good things take
      their time, stop
      for coffee on the way,
      get lost. turned off
      their locations.
      i've been waiting
      on my front steps for years.

iv.   jennifer says i call men beautiful
      and expect people to just take
      my word for it.
      i guess i don't know
      another adjective to give
      the men who get me like summer
      asphalt's hot breath after rain.
      i guess if i started saying

i've met a lot of men
who looked like answers
people'd start to wonder just how many
problems i have.

v.   every fictional character
i've ever had a crush on is probably
a sagittarius
and some things
are beyond fixing.

vi. there's never really a right time to say
you're becoming an echo
inside your own body.

—finch greene—

dream house
—finch greene

a coat closet. floors strong enough to float the ocean in my living room. sapphire paint. plum. floral wallpaper. sheets smooth as buttercream. green velvet. mustard knit. a tall bathroom sink. white stone. silver hardware. spotless. stainless steel. virgin pipes. clear drains. neat cupboards. unexpired food. no rugs. a deep kitchen sink. whole walls. mint. lavender. no creaks. no cracks. no peel. no chip. no rust. easy to clean. no projects. elbow room for all my imagined lovers. guest beds for all my skeletons. warm lighting. no ghosts. or, no ghosts that i didn't invite in with me. a washing machine big enough to fit three fourth-graders. plenty of windows. natural light. a long desk. a mantel. a sunroom. a pantry. rooms that smell like my father making pancakes. sandalwood. vanilla. old books. a library. a ladder to reach the high shelves. a place to keep my shoes. a backyard full of birds. a cat bed in every window. some unbent peace. only touched by my hands. a welcome silence. rooms that don't ask anything of me.

to my knowledge, hank williams jr. never wrote
any songs for half-girls with complicated dead dads
  —finch greene

someone outside is playing "family tradition"
and the laundry and i
take a second to miss him out loud

i know every word in his voice,
a scratchy sweater
and a cologne for special occasions

not every bad thing left when he did—
and isn't that funny?

i vomit sweet stories and cry on the phone
to people who only know his name

i say complicated
but i just mean
mean

sometimes i only wish he was here
so i can wish he wasn't
and not feel guilty

it s hard for hate to hold
a ghost, you know

i only want to talk about
red wagons
and mountains
and country music
without tasting metal

wouldn't it be easier to pretend
that bloody mouths
are someone else s problem?

—finch greene—

How the Brain Fights Pain
  —Alexander DiFrank

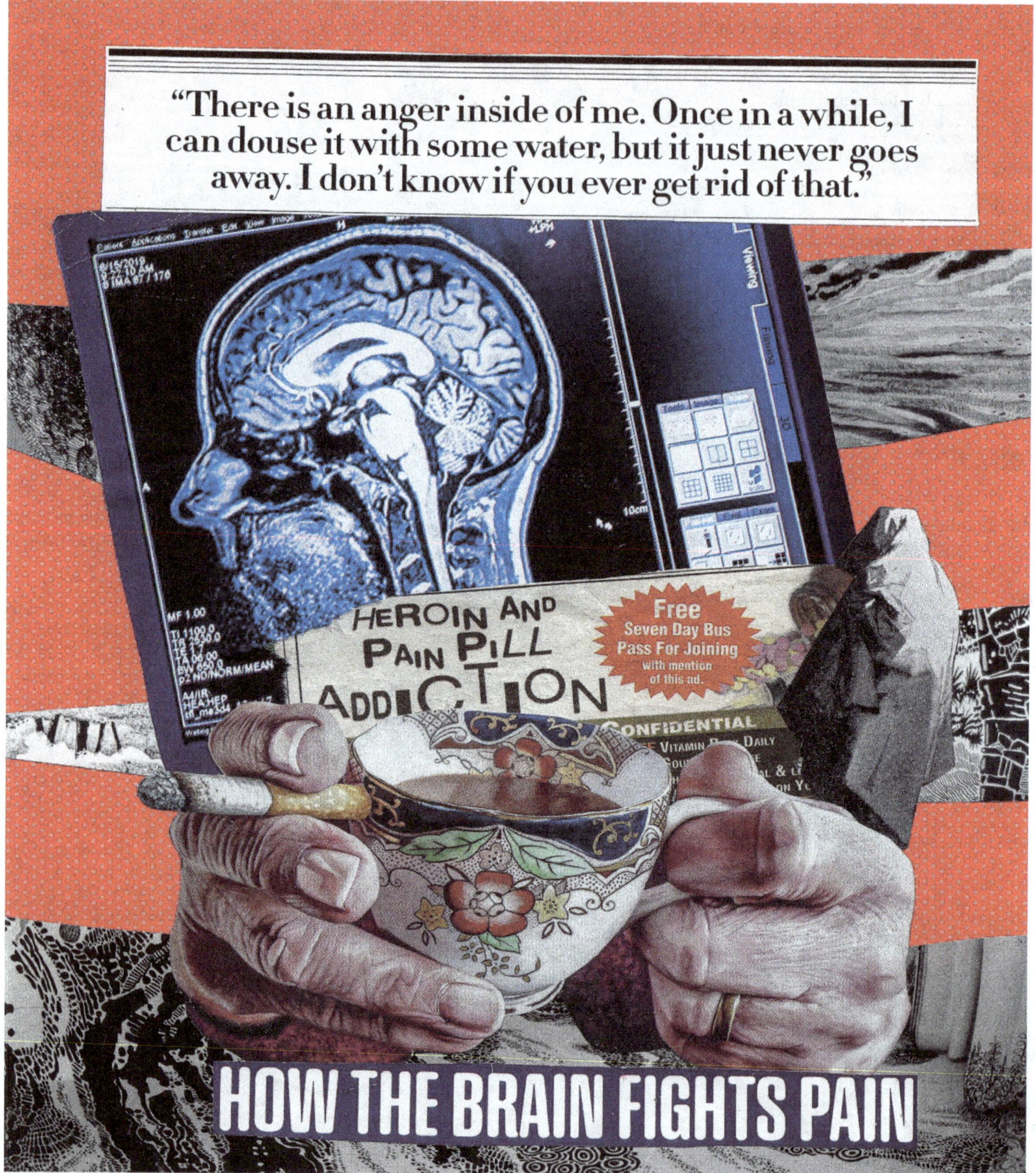

—Alexander DiFrank—

What do you think happened here?
　　—Batrisyia

Carved into time; an indoctrination of self-serving

purposes and feelings of white tombs made of limestones feeding

into submission, and birthing oppression—

a man with a dream follows a theme

of incineration on the stake;

the masonry conveys a hate for heresy

and the freemasons portray love for heredity.

Centuries into colonisation;

a beach cannot mask the remnants of hell—

millions of people with a need for speech

have not completely unveiled the lies they tell.

I fear for the life of me,

what's been done in that room;

pretentiously decorated with hypocrisy—

the bourgeoisie will do anything to rule.

　　I walk through the sites of holy

　　with a resentment that outlives

　　even five girls' bodies;

　　even money failed to bury such atrocities.

　　　　I felt my goosebumps rise beyond skin,

　　　　as the devil's tomb reminded me of things

　　　　that no robed men should even depict—

　　　　the eerie quiet said: trauma is present in the collective.

　　　　　　I love this anger; an unbridled pain

　　　　　　of untold stories, unheard children,

　　　　　　voices of colours that scream in vain

　　　　　　against a power that cowers from freedom.

　　　　　　　　—Batrisyia—

How Does This Affect Me?
  —*Shannon Clem*

—*Shannon Clem*—

Wallow Fragments 1
> *—Darla Mottram*

When things were going well between us, J— would bring me a yellow rose. Unknown to me at the time, he was counting them up—when he reached a full dozen he would propose. One night he surprised me while I was hanging out with friends. I invited him to come sit with us; he didn't want to, but wouldn't say so; he instead laid little traps, provocations, he knew just how to push buttons until everyone was pissed, and we went out into the night to argue. *Why are you doing this,* I asked, by which I meant, *why are you going out of your way to hurt me.* He didn't want to fight; he hated fighting; when we fought it degraded us, he said, made us less perfect. Little by little I was replacing his idea of me with the reality of me. He threw the rose on the ground, stomped on it, crushed it, told me he had been working his way towards a proposal, that I had ruined it, that there was no salvaging it now. We didn't break up that night. We hadn't even moved in together yet. I gathered the broken rose, cradled it in my lap as he drove.

—

J— and I would argue over the dumbest things, but the surface of the argument was almost always a metaphor for a deeper, ongoing conflict. Once we sat in his car outside our apartment arguing heatedly over the lyrics to "Eleanor Rigby." I heard "All the *lonely* people," while he insisted that it was "All the *lovely* people." I argued "lonely" made more sense in context: the song is about a woman, Eleanor Rigby, who stares wistfully out the window, who "lives in a dream" and the head of the church, Father MacKenzie, who is "writing the words of a sermon that no one will hear." The song ends with the woman dying and Father MacKenzie burying her and no one coming to the funeral. To me, the song didn't just use the word "lonely"—its entire aim was to convey the loneliness and disconnection of the world its characters navigate. J— told me it said a lot about me that I heard "lonely" when Paul McCartney was so clearly singing the word "lovely," that the song was about a beautiful young woman looking out the window and admiring the various passersby. He said I only read loneliness into the song because I was depressive. There: the argument wasn't about the song; it was about my deficiencies. By the end of the argument, he convinced me that I was wrong, that I was projecting my sadness onto the world once again. It wasn't until years later that I thought to look the lyrics up. I wonder what would have happened if we'd had smartphones or an internet connection, if one of us could have consulted Google in the moment and put the argument to rest. I doubt it would have changed how J— saw me, though it would have changed how he heard the song. But it might have changed how I saw myself; maybe I would have gained an ounce of trust in my own perceptions, my own ability to interpret what I hear and see. Yes, I often feel the world is a devastating, difficult place full of sadness and suffering. And it is this worldview which drives me to to create, to love intensely, to fight for liberation, and to experience joy and connection.

—

He didn't want me to go on vacation with K—'s family, whose graduation present to her was to take her and her two best friends to Dauphin Island for a few days. He was angry because we'd had a fight and he thought I should want to stay and work it out rather than going on this once-in-a-lifetime trip with my closest friends. Yet we were always fighting, and I was exhausted from it; I was also in the midst of experiencing a deep estrangement from my adopted family, and struggling to figure out where and how to live without any financial support from them. I wanted to spend this time with my friends and celebrate this next chapter of our lives; when would I ever have a chance like this again? The entire trip I was going out of my mind with worry because he kept threatening to break up with me: clearly I didn't take our relationship seriously, how could I be having a good time on the beach without him while he was at home stewing miserably over the state of our relationship? He would berate me over text and then when I tried to call, he wouldn't pick up. He didn't want to talk to me, he just wanted to make sure I felt bad. While my friends were sleeping I listened to The Smashing Pumpkins *Melon Collie and the Infinite Sadness* on repeat, lying awake deep into the night reflecting on our relationship, why it was so hard to be with someone I loved so much. Despite my misery, I missed him. I wanted to make things right, convince him that we weren't a lost cause. I gathered butterfly shells from the beach to bring to him; I washed them in the sink and then put them in a jar, all their beautiful colors on display. I wanted him to know that I'd been thinking of him, that I wanted to please him. When I gave it to him, he was unimpressed—he made a face and for some reason opened the jar, as if looking for something more, and a horrible smell wafted out. I hadn't let them dry thoroughly before putting them in the jar, so they stank. He was disgusted that I thought a jar full of putrid smelling shells would delight him. He threw them away.

—Darla Mottram—

Wallow Fragments 2
—Darla Mottram

I begin inside myself, then venture out. Walking the path at Mary's Peak there were wild irises swaying in the breeze, fog blurring the edge of the trees, little strawberries lining the paved path, and you were beside me, vibrantly alive, your tail lifting and falling, your head flung up, nose twitching far-off scents, oblivious to the future. I will always feel you trotting in front of me, a little to the right. Your presence taught me there is a world I can live inside. It exists here, this moment.

After you went, a low wind warbled through the house like a spacious bird, making it high but lonely. When you had gone the love came. I supposed it would. The supper of the heart is when the guest has gone. (Emily Dickinson). At night I miss you, and in the morning, and during the days as well. My heart grows huge feasting on this loss. E.D. again: *It is a little thing to say how lone it is — anyone can do it, but to wear the loneness next to your heart for weeks, when you sleep, when you wake, ever missing something,* this, *all cannot say, and it baffles me.*

Inside some rocks are sparkling crystals, though you can't know that without breaking them. Sometimes our metaphors are flawed. Sometimes our attempts fall short. I feel I have been "wear[ing] the loneness next to [my] heart" for *years*, you see.

As a child, I was discouraged from mentioning the past, or remembering that it existed. *I am your father now,* my adopted father said, *not that junkie who abandoned you.* He wasn't just telling me how to experience the present; he was rewriting the story of my life.

The man is the head of the household, my father said, my mother said, the church said. *Children must be seen and not heard.* I often shake with fear while speaking, but I push through the fear. The fear doesn't leave, just becomes something familiar and almost welcome, a barometer of bravery, or at least of the fact that I am still here. I was told to ask less questions, and to accept punishment gracefully. Before evening devotions, my family would gather in the living room and air our grievances: *G— did such and such; D— said _______.* The person being accused of wrongdoing would be forced to stand in front of everyone else and apologize. Defending one's actions was *having a stiff neck.* Denying them was *lying. Forgive me*, we'd say, knowing not-forgiving wasn't a choice, forgiveness therefore rendered meaningless.

I used to wake to demons hovering above me, my body frozen by sleep paralysis, a low growling issuing from my own throat. Not enough people talk about religious trauma. The difference between being *looked after* and *watched.* I learned to be constantly proving my goodness. Even as the feeling grew in me that I would never be good enough.

I do not know what I am looking for when I begin. Maybe I think I am writing you a love letter, or perhaps I am launching an investigation into my relationship to suicide, or I am only once again tunneling inside my love of language, books, where I eternally go to know/unknow myself. As a lover of this self-inflicted disorientation, it's hard to know where I am from one moment to the next. Or, as Alexis Pauline Gumbs writes in her meditation on Black feminism and marine mammals, *Most cetaceans have a crystalline lens over their eyes so they can see underwater. The South Asian river dolphins do not. Also the water moves so quickly, and is so full and turbid that not much would be visible if they were looking with their eyes. So they*

—Darla Mottram—

look instead with their voices. I think this is what I'm doing—sending my voice out in front of me to get a sense of what is too chaotic for sight, too tangled for understanding. I look by listening.

I am out with lanterns, looking for myself, wrote Emily Dickinson in a letter. Language as light in the darkness; through language I illuminate myself, make myself visible.

But I don't want to be to cling too desperately to light, to metaphors of light. Or, as Wendell Berry writes, *To go in the dark with a light is to know the light. / To know the dark, go dark. Go without sight, / and find that the dark, too, blooms and sings, / and is travelled by dark feet and dark wings.* Or as Claire-Louise Bennett writes in *Checkout-19, When everything is illuminated and the shadows have been sanitised, where goes the creature inside and what happens to her need for reverie?* I am just as interested in my unknowable self as the knowable one.

I have laid down on dark country roads to watch comets streaking against the darkness of outer space. I have walked naked into lakes at night, bats winging past, their bodies darker than the dark that holds them, drawing the power of the earth up through my submerged feet. I have danced through fields of fireflies on summer nights in Indiana, fireflies numerous as the stars that seemed to lower themselves to dance alongside us. Fireflies, plentiful in my youth, now face extinction due to habitat loss, pesticides, and the glow of artificial lights, which makes it difficult for them to find each other. Their effulgence useless without vast fields of darkness to flicker through.

At Sauvie Island, we hiked through the snow to reach the river, blanketed in fog. A foghorn lowed as a boat passed by unseen. In my memory, we stood on the shore in a circle with you at the center, all of us howling, egging you on. A video from that day reveals it wasn't a circle. I wonder at the metaphor my heart makes.

—Darla Mottram—

faceless zuihitsu, or a song for Gaza
—Liam Strong

emoticons in braille, morse code, alphabet soup with lentils, emoticons in the sagebrush for sale. we buy it like snowburn, snow like fire falling, snakes in the wind. there's many people in coffee shops, so we buy lunch hanging from cliff edges with the rest of the cattle.

/

from a distance, we can't tell who anyone is. once beyond the curvature of the earth, object permanence. once blood spills without a sound, because it so often does, then songs are written. the more names there are, the more namelessness, or so redacted from death tolls. Za'atar like crumbled roads regurgitated by kingfishers. rice in stones that were meant to just be stones.

/

the National Institutes of Health implore that if incompatible blood is transfused, the donor cells are treated as if they were foreign invaders. the patient's immune system retaliates accordingly.

/

we seek apophenia because it is human nature. which is, of course, not what we'd want to hear. we can read it on our faces. that, of course, some things have meaning. & other don't, or shouldn't. i'd like to say a prayer. i'd like to. i'd like to pray. prayer seems like praying, which seems like a thing, which seems like a thing we'd want to be effective, efficient, conducive. i want to burn a building for every person who is prayed for. but we already have nowhere to go. i'd like to say i have things i want. we want to see faces in bookshelf dust. we draw smiles in the frost lining the inside of a warming car. the images are erased, even if they're not erased intentionally.

/

shapeshifters don't want their expressions noticed. the common lycanthrope has a blood type of politician. unlike the common exile, whose body won't be recognized even if we try. anyone & everyone will be ghosts, but it doesn't feel inclusive.

/

sumac is a metaphor for fire. sumac is a metaphor for spitting tart from the mouth. sumac is a metaphor for staghorn on the run, velvet flailing from the skull, blood wanting to stay near other blood. blood needs blood to heal. a wound closes in on itself like a strip of coast woven endlessly by ocean. a scar is just a promise no one knows how to say.

—Liam Strong—

MY PORTAL TO JOY
—*Annaliese Jakimides*

—*Annaliese Jakimides*—

She told me, no one really ever dies, that the dead return as ephemera
        —henry 7. reneau, jr.

shaped from our memory of them. We want to believe, even in the muddle of
grief, that we'll find them again, in the green-dew shimmer of leaf, the crystal-
veined spider's web of ice through stone; we want the inner peace laid dormant

in the cryptic hieroglyphs of a Latin mass, despite our USA of lives are shark-
toothed, the violent, gaped mouth of capitalism, imperialism & other beasts of
Empire keeps us transfixed to the palm-glow Twitter distractions of cell-phones,

enthralled by the cult of celebrity, irrespective of the ravage of a world-wide
plague, the ever more routine wars, & viral dispossession of *Others*. The global-
I-zation sickness wrought upon *those people,* everywhere else, other than here.

Poverty's least of those amongst us, the raised fists balled tight as thrown stones.
The 24 hour news cycle—what happens to other people, somewhere *over there.*
The steel-jacketed shrapnel of foreign body intrusions, the eviscerated intestines

& compound-fractured bones that breed apathy—the tapeworm of denial that
squirms inside of its own volition, long & tangled as hunger. The blind hope as
delusional as a season of readymade scapegoats. The unaccountability,

stuttering to cover its inability to tell a believable lie, prestidigitates the velocity
of the convenient crisis & the cover-up. The dead & dying children, their small
human lives made expendable by the profit margin, prime-time ratings

of breaking news, & there are really no words for sorrow that can articulate the
unspeakable absence of God. The suffering visited upon them wanting a world
without suffering, a world where power didn't rest in the hands of

an invisible elite, & our monuments didn't only memorialize the worst of those
amongst us. Our empathy, buried inside the duct taped morality of a pantomimed
conscience, an empty beggar's cup, like someone scooping the last cup of flour

from the bottom of a cotton sack.

        —henry 7. reneau, jr.—

**Missing Persons Flyer, or the Machinery of Descent
Beyond the Diasporic Ether**
        —*henry 7. reneau, jr.*

We are constructing an explosion. Being is our combustion to
becoming, as in survival, or the subjective, both sans and

simultaneous prerogative of fable/ : a girl negotiates a night-
darkened path, disappears into an alleyway shortcut to home,

and confronts our plantation lullaby warnings of evil. In this case,
a 15-year-old Black girl named Latasha Harlins

enters a mom 'n' pop and forfeits her life. The Black body
is a mesmerizing menace, like a pagan stone fetish, like

all Black children who are murdered
are used as cautionary tales—passed away/ in the past/passed on,

like Emmett Till's story, like Tamir Rice's story, the bright eyed
innocence been Skittle-ed . . . a misunderstanding?

of how so many stories of murdered Black children
overlap. Their existence reduced to a warning. The void filled

with rage, emptiness and grief seeded in the upturned earth of
freshly dug graves,

our pain muraled on public walls. The sneakers, *in memoriam*,
strung from powerlines and loss billboard-silkscreened on T-shirts

like an arrow shot into no longer distance. The blood-splattered
ruin of Black bodies

like a scar scratched into the concrete of a sidewalk. God pointing
a gun directly at our targeted diaspora. A recontextualization?

of something *They* should not have done, or said. The footage is
obscured by

—henry 7. reneau, jr.—

the cooked narratives of a/an [im]perfect *white* world, the denials
are in the details,

the media mitigated facts, and
exoneration, of whomever is at fault. The entitled and expendable

intertwined, and language that blurs the investigation of his-story,
as the real story

is concealed in the shadows, as far from passed away/ in the past/

passed on, as possible.
But the grief and the anger, still a pulse in the city—the toxic

grounds of what used to be Empire Liquor Market, Latasha's
gravesite in Paradise Memorial Park

—passed away/ in the past/passed on, is a tragedy that words
alone cannot conciliate.

We hear someone say dead Black children
like Paradise Lost. A light switch clicked off three trillion cells

in the body, and *them* who ain't Black
act like we never existed. Like just as many stars in the cosmos

suddenly went dark. The presence of an absence—the distance
between passed away/ the past/

and passed on; *them* been murdered, as in, a lack thereof.

—henry 7. reneau, jr.—

Family Tradition
    —Maria Pianelli Blair

—Maria Pianelli Blair—

Skeletons on the outside
—Belea

I started wearing skeletons on the outside

when I was only about ten years old.

By that I mean I was fascinated

by the raw image of my bones perking out of my body.

I think it's a common thing for people like me

whose flesh covers up the innards so much

that it's hard to cover them up later, with clothes.

And no one says that our ribs show.

At ten years old, it seems so important

to have a couple of floating protuberances

shaping the ribcage

peeking through the skin, when it is not loaded.

It's curious, or bizarre (if you haven't been through it)

that someone would want to tear their flesh

to reveal the ivory and the blood

but I've been haunted by that craving ever since.

It is often said that the weight shelters

and supports all the falls, and we put on garments and garments to protect our lives.

We believe by association that weight

acts as a lifeline but it is not true

and we forget that the impact is not softened

under the fat and the thickness and the breadth

and that the skeleton under everything is forgotten.

Wearing skeletons on the outside comforts me.

It doesn't just remind others that underneath the flesh

I am me, a person, sentient, suffering,

but it also gives me a little nudge:

"Hey, be careful, I might break,

and if I break, your guts and blood will spill out

and, of course, so will this beating heart,

and I won't be able to take care of them anymore if I break."

I look at the fabric of the clothes with vinyl bones

with a certain tenderness after so many years.

So much time has passed and so much comfort has come to me

that I feel I already have two skeletons:

      one on the inside

           and the other on the outside.

—Belea—

Yarn Poem 188 (found years)
   —John Rodzvilla

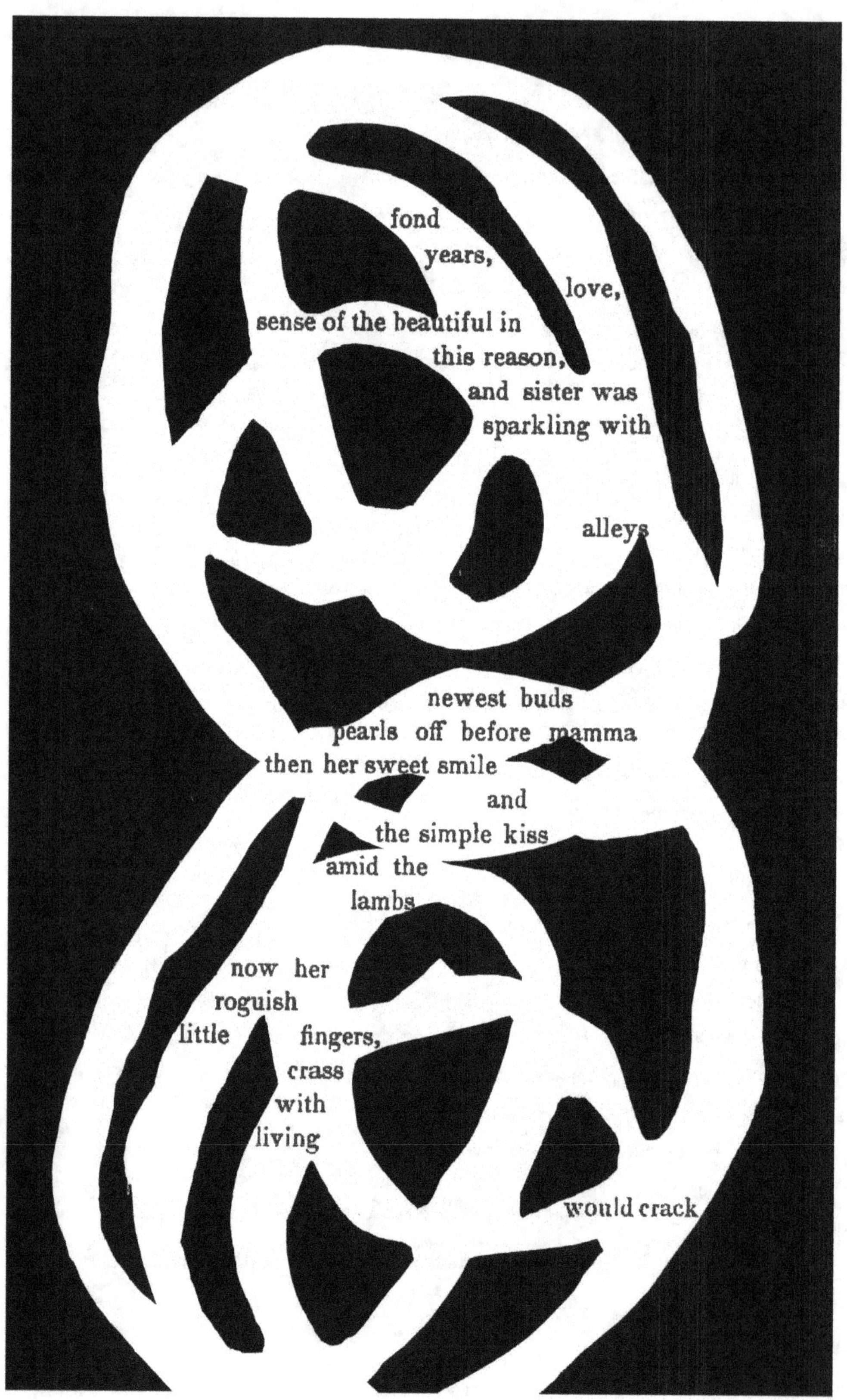

—John Rodzvilla—

Yarn Poem 204 (golownin)
　　—John Rodzvilla

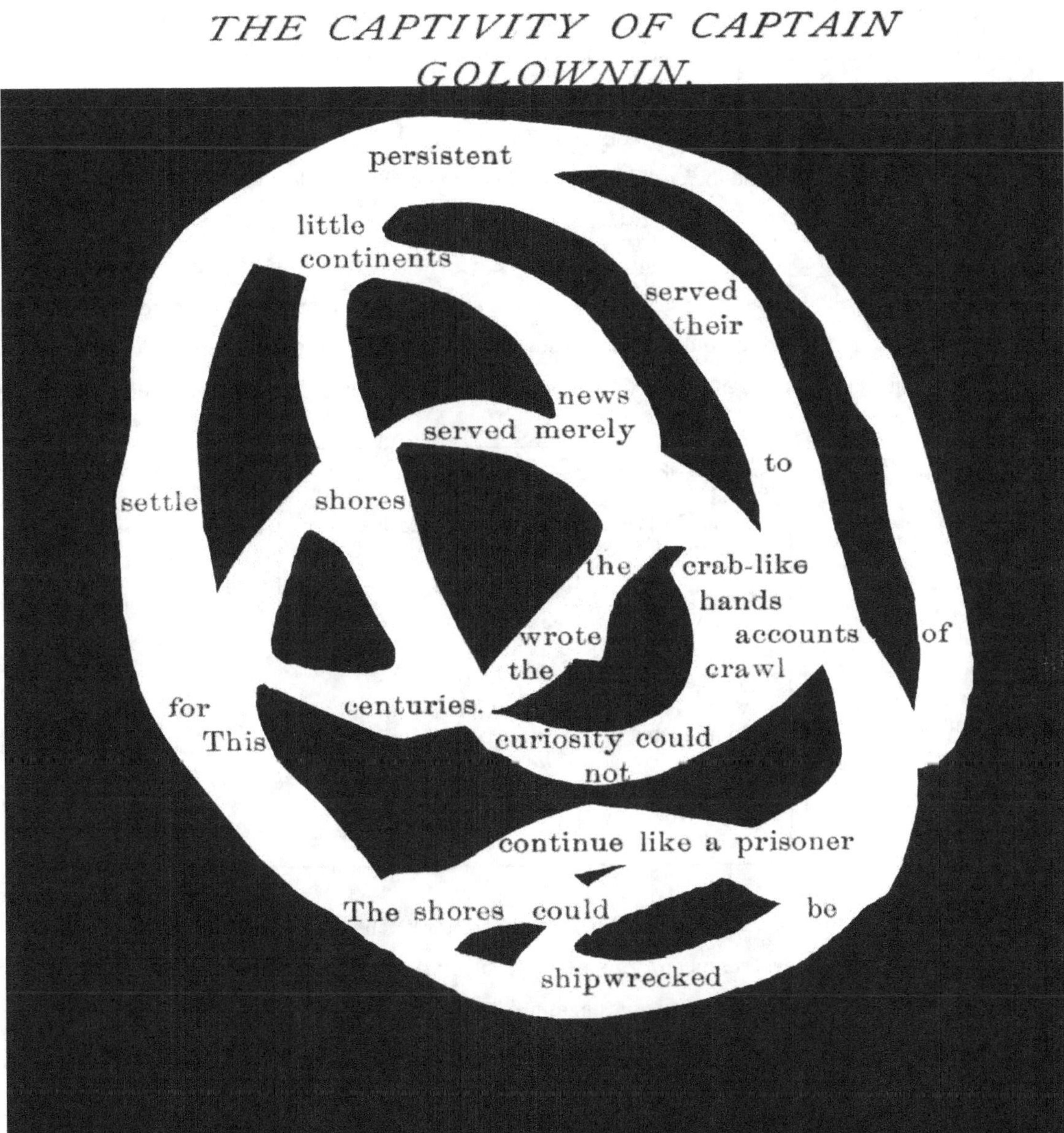

—John Rodzvilla—

The Non-Human Family's Somber Narrative of the Nameless Alien Animal and Its Body and Its Burial

after Christopher Soto, with love

—Callie Jennings

And by "myself," I mean where my attention usually catches. I overslept and cracked a glass and bled onto the shimmer blouse in bone, so I bought flowers for myself. Vase crowded as a triad in a twin bed. I loved the flowers, and then I forgot them, and then they changed and I didn't see, and then I saw and didn't want to see, and then I was ashamed of seeing the change, and then I hated the flowers. Then I swept the fallen petals, and then I shooed the midges. I looked into the worry cabinet and in its mirror corridors saw flowers and flowers and dollars for flowers and flowers too dead, again, and the cost of the death and the counting to death and the death. After such expense to cross the expanse between alive and *alive*, after such a cost of living, after costly dying, all its flowers, there is some point beyond which nothing more will change. By sufficiently objective measures every outcome is the same. I stopped buying flowers for myself. Then the flowers brittled to cold sepia and I loved that they didn't pretend to life or growth. I loved the mantel swept and midgeless. Then nothing changed forever. Then I loved the flowers.

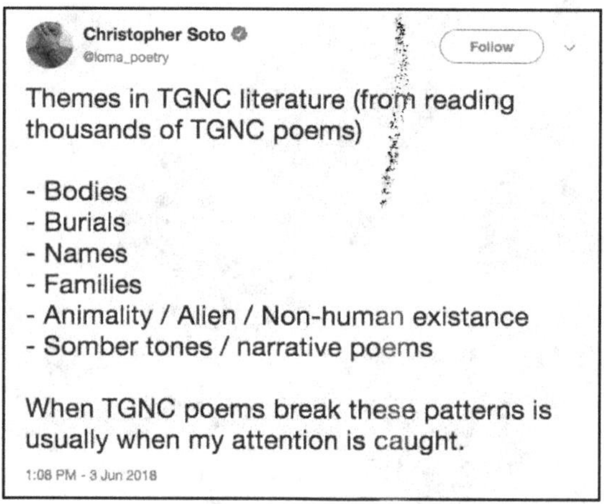

It happened, just this way, the flowers. What's the word for when you are a metaphor but for the opposite of what you need to mean? This is my problem: in my family we were taught to love our enemies and here a family of enemies is in my bedroom—dead flowers, fixed text, a family of fast machines stapling waving stigma down, lying like a family system. A page that presses is neither true nor false. I mean to roil blues and rules like a covered steady boil. Spidering spillage. I mean to wash in steaming shout then dry then be tucked into the spine between alive and *alive*. Go away. Away from my hollering clouds of midges, away from my first degree name. If only I could tumble down a mountain, buried in the belly of a wolf, and fill him full of pummeled song, its taste unsavored. If only I could make a single sandwich that's not a trans body. If only I could break apart, I'd break into a thousand thousand silly lyric literatures, pistils whipping in the wind. But I am bound, unread, so every brown and broken brittled pattern stays *alive*. You can't have me. Don't touch me. Now touch me. Take me. And by me, I mean my attention, caught fire.

—*Callie Jennings*—

the trouble with holding
—Callie Jennings

an ice cube to my nipple is I can't get off with cold hands. the trouble with a glove is melting ice soaks through. the trouble with chopsticks is no purchase. the trouble with ice tongs is what kind of bougie kitchen maven do you think I am. the trouble with popsicles is they make me think of sticky children I won't have. the trouble with M is they left for Oregon. the trouble with J is I don't know how to apologize for saying someone's pussy tastes like One Direction. The trouble with the other M is I don't know how to apologize for giving head to One Direction and saying the One Direction is *on my tits*. the trouble with a rando from trans discord is first I'll have to listen to her DJ or listen to her reenact her last therapy session as standup or listen to her cry about how lonely she is despite me being right damn there or all the above. the trouble with Fetlife is have you ever been to the internet. the trouble with clothespins is they were my mother's. the trouble with leeches is wow I can't believe my brain went there but I kind of want to try it but where do you get a leech that's definitely negative for swamp diseases. the trouble with ordering nipple clamps from Etsy is I don't know how to tell what's made with child slavery. the trouble with ordering nipple clamps from anywhere is can the wilderness take the components back, where was the metal mined and how, whose death might I be ordering. the trouble with my nipples is they're helping to bring about a second American civil war. the trouble with coming is I need to be lying down. the trouble with lying down is all land is stolen land. the trouble with lying down is there are lives at stake. the trouble with lying down is someday and soon I will lie down for the last time and forever. the trouble with pleasure is how many years I went without it and there's no way to get the years back. the trouble with pleasure is if it's a bottomless well, I'd still jump in because falling makes my hair look pretty. the trouble with pleasure is it's a good or service I can't tell the price of. the trouble with loving yourself first is what even could that mean if not consumption. the trouble with love is what even could it mean if not consumption. the trouble with meaning is what is there but consumption and production for the purpose of it. the trouble with meaning is what we're really saying is location in an economic system. the trouble with the concept of an economic system is by system we mean what affects and is affected and there is no levee for economic effects and so it's everything, it's all of everything, changes in migrations and the composition of the atmosphere, what we give up for gauzy illusory safety, knives and winter and giraffes and strangers' homes and the moons of other worlds, like Ganymede, bigger than Mercury, more water than Earth, most beautiful catamite moon, gay as in tragedy, gay as in victim, gay as in godlike to gods, armored from Jupiter by a hundred miles of ice hiding ocean hiding ice hiding ocean of most precious innocent free-flowing moon water, organic, salty, an unlabeled landless aloneness to float in, float effortless up toward the ice, nipples first.

—Callie Jennings—

Day 0.

—Paula Urdaneta

Today I want to be
the shudder that
lies beneath our skin:
bodies clasped together in the night.

I know I'll never belong to the rain
nor the merciless sun.

Today I want to be the whirlwind
that pulls the air out from windows
that topples houses and
is gone.
Without a home.

Today I want to be his.
I want to be the teeth
that scrape across my nipples
the tongue that runs through the folds
between my legs
the trail of spit left behind
the pain gathered in my womb.

Today I want to be more than
this longing for my mother.
I want to be the fingers that
unravel in clothes.

I want to be something more than
the pain of leaving
the boiling of an involuntary scream.

I want to be more.

I want to be my own.
The clarity of my footsteps in the night
the dispossession of the soil
a mass of throbbing flesh
that cries out

and is.

—Paula Urdaneta—

So You'll Have to Work Just a Little Bit Harder
    —Lucien Rae Gentil

—Lucien Rae Gentil—

Whore Poetica
—Kelly Gray

The younger poet said: you don't see the word whore in poetry very much. That's when every pen started leaking that tilted, leaning word, the W and H moving towards the end. The sound of oar, the whore river. The whore rose. The whore daisy. Those scrappy busted knees with ease. Whore me. I will mark the word in every book. Whether writing about deer or fabric. Whether writing sonnets or epistles. Weather made of whore. Dear whore. Dear whore, with your neat bed and salted collar bone. Dear whore, with my resentment caught between your breasts. Dear whore, can you hear me sing. My voice an alleyway, a pot of stew, a new car. The year is 1959 and you can smell the word Cadillac like gold, like currency, like a whore blizzard on a long highway and the radio comes in smooth, her neck glowing from the dashboard lights, the coyote caught as if on screen, that grand cinema of a late night drive, the dress hitched up, and those whore knees, which are mine if you don't believe it is too late to change our point of view, leaning.

I Ran into You at the Checkout Line after Having Left My Daughter in the Car
Or, A Study of Archetype at Trader Joes
—*Kelly Gray*

I was wearing the dress that pops open if I walk
with my shoulders back, saying, I suppose, that if I am worthy
of any space at all
then look at all of me,
at my dime store bra (the color of armpit)

and at the pinpricks of black speckled skin draped across my clavicle.
Draped, because it is fabric like, deep creases catching sun,
giving way to a field of white snow body. Not a new snow body,
but old snow, behind the trailer snow,
dirt snow where you might find piss snow.

I had a cart full of groceries, a selection well past caring what people think,
canned biscuits *this* and birthday cake for no occasion *that.*
The tallest item was an orchid, snatched from the front of the store
where a line of women my age stood
picking them up and putting them down like some sort of holy act

where we balance our interior economies against a banner of memes
texted to us by friends who claim that pleasure is healthy,
like gut bacteria, like sleep, like a revolutionary act
as opposed to a biological eventuality.
Like you ringing up my groceries

while asking, *Do you like these flowers,*
and I say, *Yeah I like these flowers,*
but I don't know if I twelve-dollar like these flowers.
And that's when you move them across the scanner
low enough not to register the bar code.

On the drive home I try to remember who said
that every person you see in your dream is a version of yourself,
but decide to think of it this way:
what if every man in my life is a version
of me. Could I walk through the store naked then.

—Kelly Gray—

Could I stop eating meat then.
Could I meet you on the rock and uncoil the snake
I found when I was ten, give myself a new name
that you will never say,
not in this language that we both have

caught between our lips,
but rather hold my name
with both hands
like an overripe persimmon
or a fragile dying rabbit brought in from the rain.

—Kelly Gray—

Found Poem on the Goddess Persephone
   —Zoraida "Ziggy" Pastor

Because she ate one pomegranate seed, she is doomed to their own country.
It happens year after year, just as the grassy hills turn blond.

You cannot put this into the orderly package of an anecdote. Persephone,
abandoned to her own country, thinking about Aphrodite, and hoping for:

Love. Simplicity. Kindness. For *He* lived as simply and as untroubled as a goldfish.
He sat in his chair, ate, what happens next is a violin solo,

meanwhile, the outside goes on, blanketed in the snow-white
tears of her mother, Demeter, impotent.

The silence of *his* house was a living thing. It wrapped itself around her.
When asked how they got along,

Persephone said, "We got along well, considering
his house was always on fire."

—Zoraida "Ziggy" Pastor—

Snails and a Child
—*Erika Lynet Salvador*

—Erika Lynet Salvador—

Vulture and a Woman
        —*Erika Lynet Salvador*

—*Erika Lynet Salvador*—

Fungi Forest
—*Erika Lynet Salvador*

—*Erika Lynet Salvador*—

Large-leaved lupine

  —jessamyn duckwall

apex   —There are wolves in the long taproots, holes in the leaves,

blade   —cuttings in the lungs that might not take. Each dried seedpod

vein   —I open, the rattling sound gets lost inside, somewhere

midrib   —rib-dark. I may never own such a flower. Yet I am bound to it,

stipule   —its entire. When sleeps frays, wolves. The devil and its batwing

node   —lobed, roseate. I change my tongue into a petal, let it

stem   —uncloud, disembark. When it withers, wolves. What draws the eye

sepal   —to any given, silent thing / what coheres in this dim world?

petal   — Perversion: mutant: hooded wing

pistil   —cradling a keel, fast inside. I take the devil in my chest,

style   —turn him to a bee, abdomen covered in a dusty bloom.

ovule   —I will keep him sexed and wretched like a metaphor. See these demon- horns

ovary   —crowning me? I've grown new parts, adornments for this

( )   —pupal, seraphic body. My howling palms unfurl to reap what has been sown.

—jessamyn duckwall—

Inheritance

—jessamyn duckwall

I ghost inside the house when the sun shines. They say
the rooms of the mind are reflected in the rooms

of the house, but what of the garden brandishing
its high, invasive arms? The choked and shadow-

drowned tomatoes. When I go outside I can't
even look at the greenish ruins I've constructed.

and I am in them.

When it's too hot for dog feet on pavement I drink
beer instead of water and dream of grizzly bears

—wake sweated through and sticky, smelling like bread.
A little salty sweet. Have to wash fish piss

from my hair after swimming and I don't water
the plants; spiders nest in their shade, spiders and june bugs.

I am making slug traps I am scattering eggshells.
Wonder what my gramma would say about this mess.

She liked dahlias and pretty things like that.
I think I shame her memory sometimes when there's

dishes in the sink. I used to wash her dishes
when she got too sick to stand. She always was

a good gardener. She worked hard in the heat
and carried beer in a small blue cooler.

Girlhood as dark magic

"I once was lost but now am found, was blind but now I see"

—jessamyn duckwall

Once was a girl
born in a church
and given

        gifts (bright
        wounds) too
        large for one

small body.
Once sang of
the blood, its graces.

        Baptized in a river,
        baptized
        in a basement,

in the dark—
I had to fill my
god-hole, quiet

        its howls, feed
        its hungry mouth.
        Once was

harlot,
was jezebel and
marked so.

        Once was a girl
        given meth for sex
        by an older man

(twenty-four to
my own
sixteen). With him,

—jessamyn duckwall—

        his crystal ball, darting
        tongue, I
        pretended

it was my idea.
Sweating out of my
clothes, flying through

        the ash-dark, ash-stale
        house on wings of
        light, my meth eyes

spinning fearsome halos,
words falling from my mouth
the way I imagined

        speaking in tongues
        was supposed to
        feel—

Now wearing only
a stranger's
white t-shirt I watched

        the smoke about my head
        vanish like the holy ghost. Felt
        the wolf fenced in

my ribs close
its mouth and sleep.

—jessamyn duckwall—

Bug Mouth
   —Savi

—Savi—

That Feeling When Time Stops and Everyone Listens
—Hannah Love

There's a guy who comes to the neighborhood to visit his girlfriend and they sit in the back of his pickup and he plays a banjo and she smokes a cigarette and the people walking their dogs slow their pace and the grannies gardening their front yards pause for a moment, handfuls of earth suspended in mid-air.

Time unzips itself from the crowd like a jacket that's too tight on too warm a day and the sighs and the sobs and the tickles of premature laughter stir more freely in all of us. The longer we stand there listening, swaying, nodding our heads, the deeper we all sink into rest and rhythm. The banjo is no longer just a banjo but a drum, the cigarette smoke incense binding us together in a brief respite from the world.

A dog barks and the sound of metal striking rock cries out as one of the grannies digs her trowel back into the ground and the guy kisses his girlfriend goodbye and drives away.

The neighborhood moves on.

—Hannah Love—

Gatsby Erasure
  —Justin Hocking

THE GREAT GATSBY   153

the picture and anybody would have said that they were
conspiring together.
    As I tiptoed from the porch I heard my taxi feeling its way
along the dark road toward the house. Gatsby was waiting
where I had left him in the drive.
    "Is it all quiet up there?" he asked anxiously.
    "Yes, it's all quiet." I hesitated. "You'd better come
home and get some sleep."
    He shook his head.
    "I want to wait here till Daisy goes to bed. Good night,
old sport."
    He put his hands in his coat pockets and turned back
eagerly to his scrutiny of the h   presence
marred the sacredness of   and
left him standing there   moon   er
nothing.

—Justin Hocking—

Aftershaft

—*Dia Van Guten, Art by Katy Somerville*

The convertible is white on white—an ivory paint job and a tattered ragtop. The wings lower, tucking into the bird, and I rise up from the passenger seat. I ride in the clouds, no car seat, no seat belt, *standing.* Dad is a god behind the wheel, but he exits the car and it slips out of park before he can unhook the barbed fence. *Dia! Get down!* It happens too fast. A farmer takes us to see his wife. She sops the blood, a warm wash of red, and prays. *Jesus, please. This little face.* I learn her language—the word ojo, two eyes with a nose—and I learn her fear. She has a big hairy wart. I'm in the clutches of a fairytale witch. I leave my body to float behind the lazy boy. From up there, she's a kind old woman bent over a lucky trickster with one unpeeled cheek. Two eyes still, but just barely.

—Dia Van Guten & Katy Somerville—

Lost & Found
—Katie Cohan

winterlost

too old for snowmen, the young woman takes

a handful of snow, presses it into the damp bark of a dying tree with frozen fingers.

her eyes give off a light that bounces off the blank landscape,

ricocheting towards slumbering birds, startling their feathers.

she has no concept of her radiance.

he crouches nearby, elbows-to-knees, glances left.

suddenly stands, kicks at the snow until shivering dirt pieces fly from the ground,

raining on her red shoes.

he tries to explain. he talks far too much.

he does not know her brilliance.

"i am no longer here," she gasps.

steam curls roll off her lips,

she begins to breathe out.

summerfound

her friends claim she died after being

struck by lightning bugs.

they swarmed, held tightly to her clothes,

carried her up into the sable sky.

her shoes slipped off, tumbled through ice air.

they were discovered on a miry riverbank, scarlet & tattered,

the only evidence found.

i might know better…

leather skin now embraces her bones,

her smile forever forward-fixed,

laughing at her skipped heart.

after all, lightning bugs can't survive the cold.

once upon a time, a lover, a madman

cried "but baby, i love you!" while

lunging forward,

—Katie Cohan—

—Katie Cohan—

silencing a breath,

quieting a life.

with each fit of rage, an ancestor's eyes shut tightly,

a grandchild wails,

a sigh echoes outward…

and for those of us searching,

each polished femur,

chipped tooth,

broken wing,

is nothing but

precious.

—Katie Cohan—

EVERYTHING I HAVE SCAVENGED IN MY BACKYARD
—*Sarp Sozdinler*

problem set 1689[1]

—Sophie Farthing

1. The woman had safely stored away one hundred and seventy-four positive memories of her father. She had also stored x number of memories that she tried not to remember. Is x greater than or equal to the total positive memories saved? Solve for x to determine whether this woman really had something to cry about.

2. Seven thousand and three-hundred-odd days I lived with you. I am sorry that

3. A small girl bends over a bed to be punished because she drove her brother's tot car over the leather sofa again. She screams over the buzzing in her ears, and her arms and legs twitch and skitter against the star-patterned quilt. Her nose drips. The girl is between 4 and 6 years old, and her father is between 34 and 36 years old. This man says that he will strike her *ten* times, but the child hears *one hundred*, and she sobs to herself, "That's too many!" Should the girl stop being melodramatic after the difference between *ten* and *one hundred* is explained? What *is* the difference between *one hundred* and *ten*? Hint: CPS, bruises, the man's self-esteem.

4. Divide a guardian's sexual comments about a minor by the innocent intent of the guardian. Multiple the quotient by {physical threats + financial dependency + [silent treatment x (expressed discomfort + criticism of guardian's personal opinions on beauty products and fashion)]}. Remember to factor in the guardian's concern that bad men would perceive the minor as a sex object if the minor wore skirts above the knee.

5. Your dad yelled at you because you talked back, now you are hiding in your room, you are shaking all over, and you can't breathe. You know that you must apologize to your dad for being sassy or he will glare at you and your mom will look disappointed. However, you feel physically ill. How many minutes should you wait before choking down the nausea and leaving the room to face your sneering father? Record your answer to this problem in units of shame.

---

[1] Note: This piece is inspired by Charles Jensen, *Story Problems,* 2017.

—Sophie Farthing—

Just Fooling No Need To Stare
—*Sean "Disgusticator" McGarry*

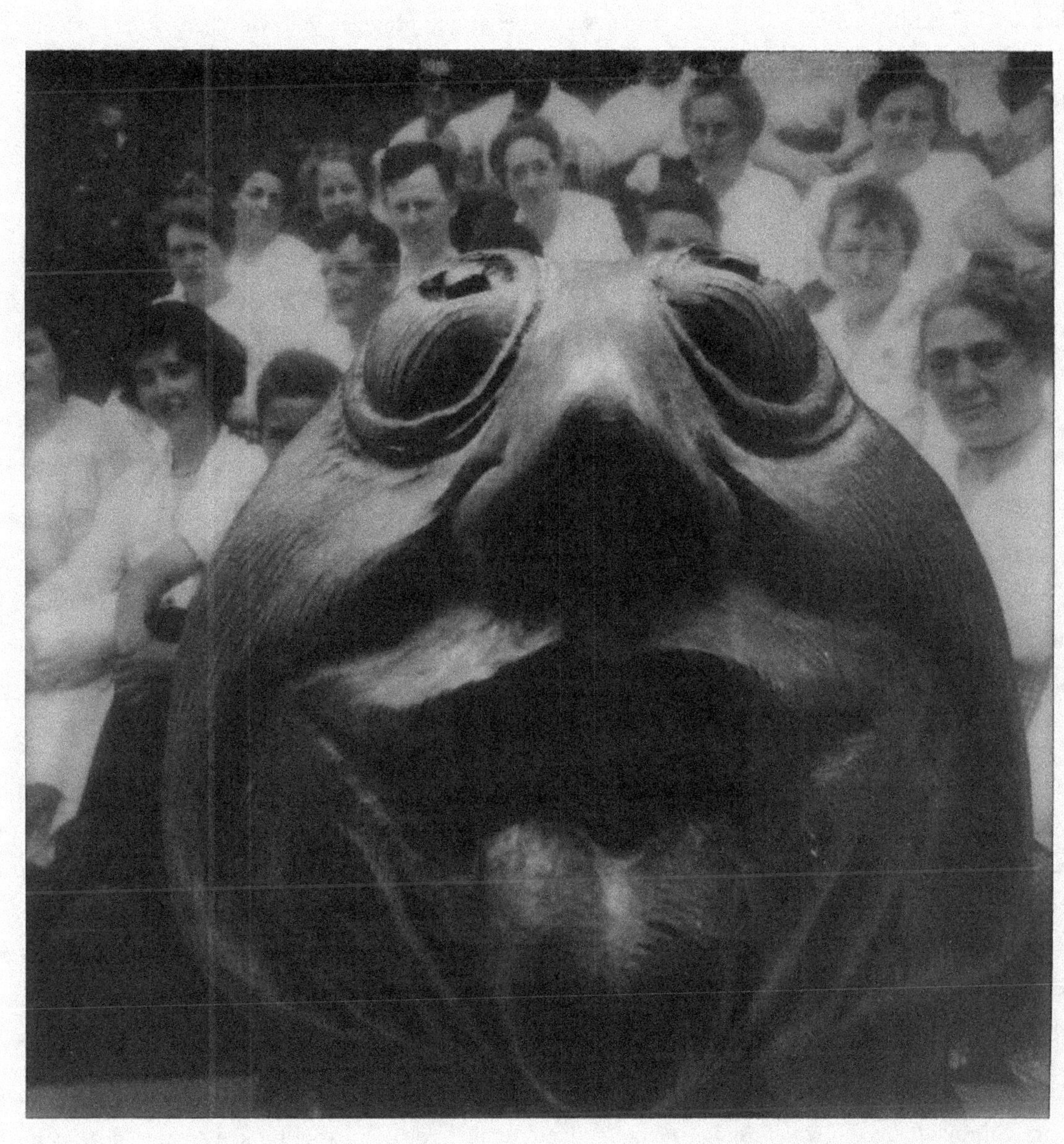

—*Sean "Disgusticator" McGarry*—

The Viable Humster

—Lino Heissenberg—

There are a few vital things you need to consider if you want to be comfortably sad. For example, you should make sure to switch the lights off, because a dark room isolates way better and provides you with that particular feeling of being alone, but not alone in the universe, because you are aware there are people outside your dark cave, but they are not here: That way, it feels as if it were you, and only you, who is alone, and that is deeply alone, and that helps strengthen the sadness. It's important to let no one know you're doing this, lest they drag you out of your room, which is warm and safe and lonely, out into the light, cold and uncaring and full of people who prefer to be lonely in groups.

In December of 1938, in East London, nearby the Indian Ocean coast, museum curator Marjorie Courtenay-Latimer, a woman with a name as if written for a novel and a keen eye for the extraordinary, ends the loneliness of the coelacanth, a fish believed to have been extinct for 66 million years, by discovering it, bloated from decompression and, for the same reason, deceased, among the catch of a local fisherman. The group of fish, more closely related to mammals, to humans, than to their ray-finned brethren, date back over 400 million years and were left alone for most of it, patiently waiting out the fifth great mass extinction and bidding the dinosaurs goodbye, and now find themselves prepared and put on display in museums, in the light, cold and uncaring and full of people who want to be lonely with them.

In addition to setting up your room, your diet needs to consist of comfort foods—which remind you that you're unwell, but not sick, not sick to the point of having a justifiable reason to be unwell—that is decidedly unhealthy. Having a cake, an entire cake, just for yourself as if that will make you feel better instead of worse, much worse, how could that not make you sad? Bake a cake if you need to. Being sad is hard, and expensive, if your favorite cake needs specialty ingredients. But it should be no less than that. Health is detrimental to the stability of your sadness, but hunger elicits action.

On the other end of the spectrum is the animal that has always been extinct and forever will be, if it weren't dragged out of all the possibilities the gene pool has to offer. The humster, a portmanteau as if uninspiredly written for a creative writing exercise about the dangers of knowledge, is a hamster's egg cell fertilized with human sperm, routinely created in labs and destroyed before it divides into two cells, but if left alone, still unviable. For the short time it is alive in the broadest sense, it is an intrinsically, fatally unhealthy being, too far removed from even the concept of health to be sad or be sad about; an unsettling scientific anecdote for the reproductively squeamish. It cannot be burdened with the task to achieve melancholy even, yet what it feels is what's at the end of the road of sadness, the road you're trying to walk down.

If, for some reason, your tear ducts have a malfunction and the relief of a quick cry is unavailable to you, you need to put in the work. Surround yourself with nostalgic memorabilia to remind you of all your broken dreams, not just the big ones, but the tiny and modest ones, to better feel the walls closing in. Remind yourself of your younger version that always suspected that you'd end up like this, and feel it watching you through the eyes of your plush toys.

Remember that book you've been meaning to write, that you actually wrote, and that no publisher was even remotely interested in, all the things you will eternally be too poor to purchase but cannot allow yourself to mourn because being materialistic would just be another character flaw to add to the collection, of that crush that never worked out because, frankly, there was never anything to work on that wasn't entirely in your head, all the crushes, honestly. Touch the remnants of the hobby you will never pick up again. Think about all the career paths now forever unavailable to you because you don't have enough life left to change course, and how silly it would look if you tried at your age. You can do it!

—Lino Heissenberg—

It's less than a one in a million chance, but it will happen, there will be this one unsupervised humster that, just a whim of fate and nature, will a) be forgotten in the lab and b) be viable, and one morning the scientists come in to check on their work and there it is, in front of them, the viable humster, and it will scream, at the top of its lungs, in pain and anger, out in the light, cold and uncaring, sad and alone, and they'll sweep that one under the rug somehow, but its scream will stay with them forever, and it will sting sometimes, the sadness of this thing, they didn't even know what exactly it was sad about, there were so many options.

But in the end, you'll break and leave the promising path to indifference you were just stepping on. The fridge is empty, or the sun comes out, or the big show you're putting on cannot warp reality enough for that one friend from another city to not randomly text you, and you book that train somewhere you didn't think about five minutes earlier, and you'll take your sadness with you on the train, but travel anywhere beyond the path threatens the stability of any mood.

It's less than a one in a billion chance, but it will happen, humans will be believed to have been extinct for about 66 million years, and suddenly one of them will have their loneliness ended, they will be dragged out of their comfortable dark cave filled with memorabilia of a life unlived, into the light, cold and uncaring, and they will scream, bloated from decompression, in pain and anger, with malfunctioning tear ducts, unable to properly express their sadness that they are not alone anymore, surrounded by beings who prefer to be lonely in groups, who want to be lonely with them, and they'll break.

—Lino Heissenberg—

On Irony

—Emmanuel G. G. Yamba

Sometimes where we run towards to
avoid being missing is where we go
up in flame.

I saw violence inserting pain into the
bones of my brother for carrying a
strange face

how else could you treat a color that
resemble an enemy in your midst

even the hand he held & said,
allah yahfazuni holds its own
voice crying for salvation.

Gifts

—Ashley Sanchez

—Ashley Sanchez—

Commencement (at the School for Danger)
    —Ceridwen Hall

The world you've prepared for no longer exists once you reach it. Forget like the wind if you want to survive. Boats flip, fevers strike etc. and if you make a fortress of the mind, it will always need defending. Try instead to outgrow the siege, then the recession and other linear calamities. Some bridges you must cross every day of your life. Others only once and fast; some you tread, some you watch crumble. Stories too must be engineered and destroyed, or reinforced with concrete details— eucalyptus, sun-rash—and various small denials. Every skeleton has her own closet of hush within muscle and habit. Because the best disguises are entire lives. Fail here, fail hard. Scatter your shed teeth, your old truths. Stay awkward and irreconciled to the strange fibers of time— call this grace, call it viscera—let swing the between brain and ghost.

—Ceridwen Hall—

(Re)assembly
—*Ceridwen Hall*

The social equivalent of playing
dead is to put forward a façade—

—Nuar Alsadir, *Animal Joy*

a strange mirror animal emerging from my stall into the blow-dried buzz, then the pulse of music, I blink and blush, never could stand the waxiness of lipstick, or the carbonated taste of small talk. Names drip and drop. In theory I: nod-and-smile my way through the deluge, shout my lines when told by the loudest to speak up. My voice, nondomestic and inclined to stealth, grates in my throat. A school of fish batters my skull—school: a blurring of noises and rivalries, bodies and thoughts, where every utterance requires decoding. The creature in my brain freezes amid everyone's polite swaying. I arch my spine in self-approximation, inhabiting a social body—

that flies under the radar in order
to ensure the survival of the True Self

as the crowd cheers and swarms. From this distance, I see a flag near the door, hanging still, as if to demand a pledge

—*Ceridwen Hall*—

Maggots
—*Daniel Schulz*

I spent more time outside of my apartment
than in it. I spent more time waiting tables

than studying. I spent more time sleeping
at the train station than in my own bed.

The blanket remained wrinkled, unfolded,
unlike my work shirts, constantly starched.

Every day was a cocktail stain spread across
the week. Train tracks rolling under my eyes,

until I became the skeleton crew of labor
at my work place. My boss barking orders at me,

licking the palm of his customers. Good dog,
eating away at his own work force. More shifts

for me. More money. Until my body burnt out
like the cigarettes I was smoking, turning my mind

into a haze, a fog so dense that when it finally dissipated,
my brain was as worn out as my apron. Tossed in the can.

I quit. The first time in months I could sleep in my bed
without the alarm clock ringing. The first time in months

I no longer worked eight to twelve-hour shifts. Weekends
were free again. The first time I noticed the stench

inside my kitchen. Opening the door was like excavating
a rotting corpse. Pots full of maggots, flies on the wall.

My job having eaten me up
from the inside-out.

—*Daniel Schulz*—

Imagined Scene of a Childhood Dream
    —Sean "Disgusticator" McGarry

—Sean "Disgusticator" McGarry—

I sense I am only increasing your annoyance
    —Victoria Spires

So when I need your *didaktik*, I'll

tell you. Meanwhile,

dust armies,

false equivalence,

incomparably large

intellect?

revenant

behaviours,

relentless

questioning as a power

play, relentless questioning as

foreplay, convenient

bodies, cosmic

fault lines, clumps

of matter,

tiresome self-

abnegation,

the cold

certainty of

winter stars,

defiance in

passivity, personal growth,

et cetera.

—Victoria Spires—

Melt

—Sam Moe

You try not to look at her but you can't help it, the magnetic pull of the evening too much for you to withstand, everyone melting from the first heat of winter, air vents blowing particles around the living room like bits of snow, there is wine and there is laughter, there is alcohol in lime green bottles and appetizers glazed with sugar, a dash of salt, you are on the couch furthest from me, I can't tell if your boredom leads you to desire, to devour, or if this is another party trick, know you put on such a cute personality for the others, this won't end well so I pretend to be her, imagine what it would feel like to glow from within, to wear boots to dinner with ripped jeans, a crushed pack of cigarettes, I excuse myself to the bathroom so I can make faces in the gilded mirror, the wallpaper behind me is full of purple parrots, I get lost on the way back, I am greedy, would turn into your favorite dessert if you asked kind enough, instead we avoid each other, you know too damn well these days I'm a warning bell, you're a gem, you prefer dimly lit hallways of dust and fire, you only love when someone is covered in distress, so I distract myself with the blood-red rocks glasses and soft-billed pelicans stamped on the ceiling in the dining room, heron feathers made of glass dangle from the chandelier, no one can figure out if I twist my stories or my heart into lies, someone asks if I'm going to write about the evening and I respond by eating all the ice in the freezer, later you'll ask if I'll sit next to you and I'll try, really, to pretend I don't have a soul, a body, no blood in my veins, I am a ghost spore, you might trap me in a jar.

Biographies

Alexander DiFrank (he/him) is a 25 year old collage artist. Alexander had been dabbling in different forms of art since he was a kid. However, he ended up finding the most catharsis in collaging. He finds that being able to dissect his feelings through scraps of paper and a glue stick has been incredibly beneficial for his mental health. Alexander's work typically focuses on topics of mental health, substance abuse, relationships, and sexuality/gender identity. You can find more of his artwork on instagram @alxxande. Alexander's piece, How the Brain Fights Pain Copyright information: Brain imaging photograph- Robert Clark, from January 2020 issue of National Geographic ; Hands holding tea - "Barbara" by Jackie Sandelands-Strom ; Black and gray bits in the background - "Paraiso", 2018, by Oscar Oiwa Copyright Oscar Oiwa Studio

Alexandria Piette (she/her/they/them) is a resident of her birthplace, Grand Rapids, Michigan. She is the indie author of The Blazing Heart of a Moonlight Arsonist. They enjoy literature and poetry, viewing the numerous seasons of Supernatural on repeat, and caring for their hellion cats, Rue and Winston.

Writer/mixed media artist Annaliese Jakimides's work has appeared in print, audio, and performance venues nationally and internationally. Her life has been lived at the intersection of inner city (pop. 650,000) and rural town (160). Nominated for the Pushcart Prize and Best of the Net, she's been a finalist for the Stephen Dunn Poetry Prize and the Maine Literary Awards in poetry and nonfiction in multiple years. Included in many journals, magazines, and anthologies, her work has also been broadcast on NPR and Maine Public. New ekphrastic fiction will be published in the forthcoming anthology The Memory Palace. She is a contributor to the musical Love Affair, premiering summer 2024. She lives in Maine. @annaliese_jakimides. annaliesejakimides.com

Ashley Sanchez (she/her) is a collage artist living in Portland, Oregon. She uses her trusty scissors to deconstruct used books and other printed media. Her work is expressed by taping together photos, illustrations, and occasionally typography. Most of her collage materials are collected from Free Little Libraries. Instagram - @greatest_middle_ever

Belea (they/them) is a 23 years-old Basque artist and translator whose name means "Crow". They have been interested in writing fiction and poetry since they were just starting school. Their interests include exploring the relation between nature and body and how bilingualism and diglossia affects identity, along with playing Dungeons & Dragons, taking care of cacti, reading experimental literature and drawing. Find them on instagram @crowahe

Batrisyia (she/her) started as a writer to find God and stayed a writer to thank Him. She recently graduated from her MSc in Global Mental Health, with her research focusing on decolonising resilience in Palestine and Rwanda through poetic inquiry. Batrisyia is currently exploring career opportunities to further her passion in the field; and in her free time, is working on her debut poetry collection. She firmly believes that art as resistance can change the system and liberate the collective.

Callie Jennings (@aporianautics) received the 2024 Stacy Doris and 2023 Bennett Nieberg Prizes and has work in Troublemaker Firestarter, Fifth Wheel Press, and forthcoming in manywor(l)ds, Fruit Journal, & Impossible Archetype. Her newsletter is at threemachineexpression.substack.com, and chances are she's dancing.

Ceridwen Hall is a poet and educator from Ohio. She is the author of Acoustic Shadows (Broadstone Books) and two chapbooks: Automotive (Finishing Line Press), fields drawn from subtle arrows (Co-winner of the 2022 Midwest Chapbook Award). Her work has appeared in TriQuarterly, Pembroke Magazine, The Cincinnati Review, Craft, Poet Lore, and other journals. You can find her at www.ceridwenhall.com.

Daniel Schulz is a U.S.-German writer known for Kathy Acker in Seattle (Misfit Lit 2020) and publications in journals such as Gender Forum, Fragmented Voices, Versification, Cacti Fur, The WildWord, Flora Fiction, Steel Jackdaw, The Milton Review, anthologies such as Heart/h (FragmentedVoices 2021), Get Rid of Meaning (Walther König Verlag), and his chapbooks Welfare State and No Change to Abuse (Back Room Poetry 2023). IG: @danielschulzpoet

Darla Mottram (they/she) is a poet, writer, and visual artist based in Portland, Oregon. Darla was the creator of Gaze, an online literary journal (2018-2021). Their first poetry collection, RECURRENT, is out from Querencia Press. You can find more of their work on their website, darlamottram.net, and on their Instagram (@melancholy_leopard).

Dia Van Guten writes magical realism and character focused fiction. Sometimes that character is herself. Dia's Pink Zombie Rose series has an upcoming release. Major Arcana will be published by Querencia Press.

Duna Torres Martín (she/they/fae, pen name Duna Haller) is a poet, writer, collagist and musician from Madrid, Spain. She has two poetry books out, 'Limbo' (Bottlecap Press) and 'Desierto' (Reflector Libros), as well as several poems and short stories published in various anthologies and zines.

Effie Brush (she/her), a paper and glue enthusiast, breathes life into discarded paper. She converts junk mail and magazines into art. Witness the beauty of second chances on her Instagram @piecesandpaste

Emmanuel G G Yamba writes from Monrovia, Liberia. He is a graduate of the University of Liberia, College of Science and Technology, with a BSc in Biomedical Science and the Spring Advancement Fellowship, learning writing for career advancement. His work appeared and forthcoming in SprinNG, The Shallow Tales Review, Libretto Magazine, Inkspired, Kalahari Review, Ibadan Art, TVO Tribe, African Writer, Eboquill, Nantygreen, The Light UL, Odd Magazine, WSA, World Guinness Hyper-poem record 2023, Anthology for Abunic and elsewhere.

Erika Lynet Salvador, born and raised a Filipina, is an incoming first-year student at Amherst College. Her visual art, focused on impressionism and vibrant colors using oil and watercolor, is featured or will soon be featured in the *82Review and the Quibble Lit. She also explores film and phone photography from time to time and is an avid reader of free-verse poetry. See her art at @bodeganierika or https://linktr.ee/salvadorerika.

finch greene (they/she) is a pushcart-nominated poet from the new york city area. they are a cat mom, a virgo, and very, very tired. their work has been featured in BULLSHIT lit, trash wonderland, and last leaves.

Originally from the South, Hallie Johnston holds an MFA in creative writing from the University of Miami. Her work has appeared in The Louisville Review, the Southern Humanities Review, and The Citron Review.

Hannah Love (she/her) is a woman with a laptop from Portland, Oregon. When she is not working, she is practicing creative writing and befriending cats. Her work appears or is forthcoming in Buckman Journal, Crow & Cross Keys, Across The Margin, Audience Askew Literary Journal, and elsewhere. Follow more of her ramblings on Twitter @hanniestew and Instagram @isthathannahlove.

henry 7. reneau, jr. is the author of the poetry collection, freedomland blues (Transcendent Zero Press) and the e-chapbook, physiography of the fittest (Kind of a Hurricane Press.) His work is published in Superstition Review, TriQuarterly, Prairie Schooner, Zone 3; Poets Reading the News and Rigorous. His work has also been nominated multiple times for the Pushcart Prize and Best of the Net.

Jannat Alam is finally using her real name. She edits Reap Thrill, an experimental weekly publication.

Jay Ponteri directed the creative writing program at Marylhurst University from 2008-2018 and is now the program head of PNCA's Low-Residency Creative Writing program. His book of creative nonfiction Someone Told Me is being published by Widow+Orphan House, Summer 2021. He's also the author of Darkmouth Inside Me (Future Tense Books, 2014) and Wedlocked (Hawthorne Books, 2013), which received an Oregon Book Award for Creative Nonfiction. Two of Ponteri's essays, "Listen to this" and "On Navel Gazing" have earned "Notable Mentions" in Best American Essay Anthologies. His work has also appeared in many literary journals: Dismantle, Gaze, Ghost Proposal, Eye-Rhyme, Seattle Review, Forklift, Ohio, Knee-Jerk, Cimarron Review, Tin House, Clackamas Literary Review, While teaching at Marylhurst, Ponteri was twice awarded the Excellence in Teaching & Service Award. In 2007, Ponteri founded Show:Tell, The Workshop for Teen Artist and Writers, now part of summer programming at Portland's Independent Publishing Resource Center (IPRC.org) on whose Resource Council he serves. He lives in Portland, Oregon.

jessamyn duckwall (they/she) is a queer, autistic poet from Oregon. When not writing, they enjoy reading tarot cards and talking to plants and mushrooms. They hold an MFA in poetry from Portland State University, and their work has appeared in Occulum Journal, Old Pal Magazine, Josephine Quarterly, and Radar Poetry, among other publications.

John Rodzvilla is an artist, writer, publisher and teacher. He currently teaches at Emerson College. His yarn poems have appeared in Harvard Review, gorse, and Grub Street. His work can be found at rodzvilla.com.

Justin Hocking is the author of Reclamation: A Memoir, forthcoming from Counterpoint Press in Spring 2025. In 2020 he released White Out—a collection of erasures performed on Donald Trump's The Art of the Deal. He also wrote a hybrid work of poetry and fiction entitled PS: The Wolves, and his first memoir, The Great Floodgates of the Wonderworld, won the Oregon Book Award for Creative Nonfiction. He teaches creative writing at Portland State University.

Katie Cohan (she/her) is an anthropologist, a writer, and a nature lover. She has lived in many locations and finds inspiration in learning new cultures and environments. She relates most to stories of adoptee and LGBT+ identity, connection, grief, exploration, and the natural world, so her poetry reflects these themes.

Katy Somerville (she/her) is a queer mixed media artist based is in Narrm/Melbourne. With an eclectic mix of feminity, death, and joy, she likes to make sparkly messes in her collages. She is the Art Director of online magazine, Cream Scene Carnival Magazine where the majority of her creativity and writing gets to play. Katy's artwork has been included in Not Ghosts But Spirits Volume IV (Querencia Press), featured on multiple digital magazines/publications, and displayed in a local cafe. She has also been a part of group exhibitions at Brunswick Street Gallery, Red Gallery, and Unassigned Gallery. You can spy some of Katy's art @what_katy_said

Kelly Gray is a writer and educator living in the redwoods, nine miles and seven fence posts away from the ocean. Most recently, her poetry chapbook "The Mating Calls //of the// Specter" was selected by Justin Phillip Reed as the winner of the Tusculum Review Chapbook Prize, and her writing can be found in Cream City Review, Southern Humanities Review, Pithead Chapel, Rust & Moth, and Permafrost Magazine, among other places. She is the recipient of the Neutrino Prize from Passages North, the ArtSurround Cohort Grant, and a participant in the 2023 Kenyon Review Poetry Workshop. Gray's collections, Instructions for the Animal Body (Moon Tide Press, 2021) and Tiger Paw, Tiger Paw, Knife, Knife (Quarter Press, 2022), can be found at writekgray.com.

Liam Strong (they/them) is a queer neurodivergent straight-edge punk writer who earned their B.A. in writing from University of Wisconsin-Superior. They're the author of the chapbook Everyone's Left the Hometown Show (Bottlecap Press, 2023). They are most likely gardening somewhere in Northern Michigan.

Lino Heissenberg (he/him) lives and works in Germany. He has a Master's in Fine Arts and works as an artist, writer, and curator. His body of work includes experimental video, games, installations, drawings, and prose. His works have been shown, screened, and printed in over a dozen countries, most of which he himself has not visited yet.

Lucien Rae Gentil (he/him) lives and works in Naarm/Melbourne, Australia. You can find him on Instagram @lucienraeg.

Maria Pianelli Blair is a multidisciplinary artist born in New York City and based in New Jersey. A public relations director by day, Maria spends her nights dabbling in ceramics, printmaking, embroidery, and analog collage. Her collages, fashioned on everything from cardboard to playing cards, marry contemporary imagery, found vintage materials, and magical realism. Maria's work can be found on Instagram (@sunset_sews) and Etsy. She has been published in several art magazines, including Contemporary Collage Magazine; FEELS Zine; and Photo Trouvee Magazine, among others. Her work has been featured in both galleries and virtual exhibitions, including Vayo Collage Gallery in Lyons, NY and Brassworks Gallery in Portland, OR.

Michael is an artist who specializes in both linocut printmaking as well as drawing, his practice often striving to combine the two. He holds a Bachelor of Fine Arts Degree in Art as well as a Master's degree in Art History and Visual Culture. He creates works of art depicting a variety of subject matter, ranging from still lifes, landscapes, and portraits of humans and as of late, animals. His reason for creating my prints really comes down to two reasons. The first reason is because he simply loves the process of carving into linoleum and bringing details to life, whether through block printing ink or colored pencils. His second reason is to help address and educate his viewers on a variety of subjects we face in the world today. For example, his ongoing series "Anthropocene" focuses on several endangered species and strives to demonstrate the beauty of these creatures who face numerous challenges to their lives.

Paula Urdaneta (Venezuela, 1993) graduated in Hispanic Literature and Audiovisual Journalism. Her passion for creating led her to found Colectivo Literario Solombra as a way of promoting Venezuelan literature. She was nominated in the Best Queer Performance category for the II Queer and Feminist Poetry Awards. Currently, Paula resides in the Netherlands.

Sam Moe is the author of two poetry books, with two more forthcoming in 2024: Animal Heart (3-Day Chapbook Contest) and Cicatrizing the Daughters (FlowerSong Press) and she has received fellowships from Longleaf Writer's Conference and Key West Literary Seminar, as well as writing residencies from VCCA and Château d'Orquevaux. Her work has appeared in or is forthcoming from The Texas Review, Southeast Review, Westchester Review, and others.

Sarp Sozdinler has been published in Electric Literature, Kenyon Review, Masters Review, DIAGRAM, and Normal School, among other places. His stories have been selected or nominated for anthologies (Pushcart Prize, Best Small Fictions, Wigleaf Top50) and awarded a finalist status at literary contests, including the 2022 Los Angeles Review Flash Fiction Award.

Savi (she/her) is a mixed media artist who uses pens, paper, video editing, and all types of unique audio-visual forms to portray an inner world full of controlled chaos from her neurodivergent mind.

Sean "Disgusticator" McGarry, an experimental multimedia artist hailing from Oregon, USA, merges instant photography with a variety of avant-garde techniques. With a background in psychology and social work, their art explores the intersections of perception and emotion in adventurous, thought-provoking compositions.

Shaawan Francis Keahna is a cross-disciplinary artist and writer whose works have been published in the Blood Pudding, Off Limits Press, the Vassar Review, and others. His video art has been featured at the Watermark Art Center, the Walker's Point Center for the Arts, and All My Relations Gallery. His first multimedia chapbook, MAYDAY, was published by Bottlecap Press in 2023. He lives in Baltimore, Maryland.

Shannon Clem (she/they) is a queer, neurodivergent, disabled poet residing with their daughter in California. Their work is published or forthcoming in various journals & anthologies including Beaver Magazine, The Hunger, Anti-Heroin Chic, Bullshit Lit, Warning Lines, & Not Ghosts, But Spirits Vol. III (Querencia Press). Find Shannon on Twitter & Instagram @shannontantrum & www.shannontantrum.com.

Sophia Isabella Murray is a witch, a poet, a teacher, a mother, and was once described as a Viking goddess. A comment she will happily accept as fact. Her first chapbook, The Alchemist's Daughter, was released by Time is an Ocean Press. Her second chapbook, Reasons Why We're Angry, was released in June 2023 by Querencia press. Her latest collection, Spiritual Milk, was released by Time is an Ocean Press. Prior to these publications, her work was included in several anthologies both online and in print from Free Verse Revolution Lit, The Mum Poem press, Bent Key, The 6ress, The Hyacinth Review, The Cabinet of Heed, Fragmented Voices and Blood Moon Poetry Press. You can view her work online at Instagram: @sim_poetry

Sophie Farthing (she/her) is an emerging queer writer living in South Carolina. Her work has appeared in outlets including Right Hand Pointing, Beyond Queer Words, Impossible Archetype, and Anti-Heroin Chic. Her poetry is also featured in the horror anthology it always finds me from Querencia Press. She is the winner of the 2024 Elizabeth Boatwright Coker Fellowship in Poetry from the South Carolina Academy of Authors.

Victoria Spires (she/her) is a UK-based poet, whose work frequently touches on themes of obscure philosophy, nature, and love. Her work has been featured in Flight of the Dragonfly, The Nuthatch, The Poetry Lighthouse, & Freeverse Revolution Lit. She can also be found on Instagram @jitterbug_writes.

Zoraida "Ziggy" Pastor's poems have been called "savage" by poet friends. She is a Cuban American poet, writer, and professor in Miami, Florida. Several of her poems are published in Ice on a Hot Stove: A Decade of Converse MFA Poetry, edited by Denise Duhamel and Rick Mulkey. She was shortlisted for the 2023 Slate Roof Press Elyse Wolf Chapbook prize. She is the author of Bear Echoes, a poetry chapbook sponsored by O, Miami, and The Knight Foundation. She has several poems and stories forthcoming in literary journals such as Scavengers and in Chameleon Chimera with South Florida Poetry Journal and elsewhere.